The Kingdom

The Palace

Burth

Mermaid's Cove

Crestwood

The Kingdom of Wrenly

1

The Lost Stone

By Jordan Quinn
Illustrated by Robert McPhillips

LITTLE SIMON
New York   London   Toronto   Sydney   New Delhi

LITTLE SIMON

An imprint of Simon & Schuster Children's Publishing Division
1230 Avenue of the Americas, New York, New York 10020
Copyright © 2014 by Simon & Schuster, Inc.
All rights reserved, including the right of reproduction
in whole or in part in any form.
LITTLE SIMON is a registered trademark of Simon & Schuster, Inc., and associated
colophon is a trademark of Simon & Schuster, Inc. For information about special
discounts for bulk purchases, please contact Simon & Schuster Special Sales at
1-866-506-1949 or business@simonandschuster.com.
The Simon & Schuster Speakers Bureau can bring authors to your live event.
For more information or to book an event contact the
Simon & Schuster Speakers Bureau at 1-866-248-3049 or visit our website at
www.simonspeakers.com. Designed by Laura Roode.
Manufactured in the United States of America 0214 FFG
First Edition
2 4 6 8 10 9 7 5 3 1
Library of Congress Cataloging-in-Publication Data
Quinn, Jordan.
The lost stone / by Jordan Quinn ; illustrated by Robert McPhillips. — First edition.
pages cm. — (The kingdom of Wrenly ; 1)
Summary: Eight-year-old Lucas, Prince of Wrenly, is eager to explore and Clara,
daughter of the queen's seamstress, knows the kingdom well, so they team up to find a
lost jewel and visit all of the land's main attractions as they search.
ISBN 978-1-4424-9691-0 (hc : alk. paper) — ISBN 978-1-4424-9690-3 (pbk : alk.
paper) — ISBN 978-1-4424-9692-7 (ebook) [1. Adventure and adventurers—Fiction.
2. Friendship—Fiction. 3. Princes—Fiction. 4. Lost and found possessions—Fiction. 5.
Precious stones—Fiction. 6. Kings, queens, rulers, etc.—Fiction.]
I. McPhillips, Robert, illustrator. II. Title.
PZ7.Q31945Los 2014
[Fic]—dc23
2013004771

CONTENTS

CHAPTER 1

A Secret Mission

Prince Lucas raced up the spiral stone staircase in the castle to his bedroom. He kneeled on the floor and then pulled a pile of clothes out from under his bed. There was a pair of worn trousers, a shabby shirt, a felt hat, scruffy leather boots, and a wool cloak.

Lucas had gotten the clothes for a handful of coins from a boy in the village. Now the prince stood before a mirror and tried on the hat. *This outfit will make me look like a normal eight-year-old boy,* he thought. *Nobody will ever know that I'm the prince of Wrenly.*

And that was the problem. Lucas had grown bored of being a prince. Most kids would think, *He must be CRAZY!* Lucas had everything a boy or girl could wish for: a cozy goose-feather bed, toys fit for a prince, the best cooks in the land to make his meals, and a view of the sea from the top of his turret. Lucas even had his very own horse, named Ivan. But there was one thing the prince did not have. . . .

Friends. Lucas wanted a friend more than anything in the world.

He'd had a friend once—a pretty, green-eyed girl named Clara Gills. Clara's mother, Anna, made dresses for Lucas's mother, Queen Tasha. Anna always brought Clara when she came to the castle. Clara and Lucas had played hide-and-seek and twirled on the swings in the royal playroom. But not anymore. Lucas's father, King Caleb, had forbidden it. He had said a proper prince does not play with village children. Lucas had cried until his nose got stuffy.

So day after day Lucas watched the village children walk to and from school. Sometimes they stopped at the bakery for breadsticks. In the afternoons Lucas watched the children climb trees and play tag in the

meadows. How he longed to laugh and play along with them!

And now maybe I can have friends, he thought. *Because I, Prince Lucas, have a magnificent plan!*

But Lucas had to hurry. It was

time to go. He stuffed the worn clothes into a sack and then slung the sack over his shoulder. Next he tied a thick rope to the windowsill, crawled onto the ledge, slid down the rope, and ran to the stables where he saddled Ivan. Then Lucas checked to see if anyone was around. *All clear,* he thought. He hopped onto Ivan, gave him a soft kick, and galloped away on his secret mission.

CHAPTER 2

Lucas the Brave

Lucas dashed over a bridge and down into the village. Chickens squawked and scattered to get out of his way. The villagers bowed and tipped their hats as he rode by.

Clang! Clang! The school bell rang down the lane. Lucas slapped the reins and hurried toward the sound of the bell. As he drew near, he leaped over a stone wall and came to a rest. He hopped from the saddle and quickly changed his clothes.

 Lucas tucked his curly red hair inside the felt hat. Then he grabbed a handful of dirt and smudged his cheeks. He tied Ivan to a low tree branch, and hung the sack with his princely clothes from the saddle.

"Well, Ivan," he said, "here goes."

Lucas climbed over the stone wall and stood in front of the school-house. A swirl of smoke curled from the chimney. Lucas took a deep breath. *Today I am Lucas the Brave!* he said to himself. Then he marched up to the schoolhouse and slowly pulled open the doors. *Creak!*

The children sat in front of the teacher on benches. Everyone turned to stare at Lucas. A girl with a thin braid crowning her brown hair gasped and cupped her hand over her mouth.

"Good morning, boy," the teacher

said. "Are you here to join us?"

"Yes," said Lucas. "I'm new in town."

"Please have a seat," she said. "I'm Mistress Carson. What's your name?"

"My name is Flynn," fibbed the prince as he sat down on a bench at the back of the classroom.

"Welcome," Mistress Carson said. "Class, please say good morning to Flynn."

"Good morning, Flynn," said the class.

"Now all eyes on me," said the teacher. "We're going to work on subtraction."

The children turned toward the

teacher, all except the girl with the braided crown. It was Clara, Lucas's old friend from the palace. She looked at the prince and raised an eyebrow. The prince winked at her. She smiled and quickly looked away.

Nobody seemed to notice.

Mistress Carson wrote some sums on a large slate at the front of the classroom. "Now, who would like to solve a problem at the board?" she asked.

The prince's hand shot up. He loved to add and subtract. His father had taught him math at home. Mistress Carson called Lucas up to the board. The children watched as the new boy walked to the front of the class.

I'm going to have lots of friends!
Lucas thought. Then he began to
work on one of the problems. The
room was quiet, except for the chalk
tapping on the board, until . . .

Boom! Boom! Boom! Someone

began to pound on the doors of the school. The children jumped in their seats. Lucas froze. His heart began to thump. The teacher hurried to the back of the room and opened the doors. Two burly men burst in.

Lucas dropped his chalk on the floor. *Oh no!* he thought. *The palace guards!* He wanted to run, but the doors were blocked.

"There he is!" shouted one of the guards as he pointed at Lucas. "That's the prince of Wrenly!"

Mistress Carson and the children gasped.

The other guard ran toward the prince, grabbed him by the arm, and led him toward the doors.

Clara waved as Lucas walked by. Lucas hung his head.

Now I'll never have any friends, he thought.

CHAPTER 3

Kindness Is King

King Caleb threw Lucas's peasant clothes into the fireplace. They burst into flames.

"What were you thinking?" cried King Caleb. "You are a royal prince. You must behave like one. Peasants are not equal to royals."

"But, Father, I have no friends," said Lucas. "I'm bored out of my royal britches."

"You should spend more time with my knights," suggested the king. "You can train with them."

"It's not the same," said Lucas. "I'm lonely, and I need a friend my own age. I want somebody to talk to, and most of all, someone to go on adventures with me."

The king sighed. He hated to see his son so unhappy, but he couldn't allow him to be friends with the peasants. Even *they* would think it was strange. He looked to Lucas's mother, Queen Tasha, for help.

"Your father is right," said the

queen as she brushed her long red hair. "But you are also right, Lucas. You do need a friend."

She looked at her husband.

"Anna Gills is like family to me," said Queen Tasha. "And her daughter, Clara, was like a sister to Lucas. Perhaps we should allow them to play together once in a while."

King Caleb rubbed his blond beard thoughtfully. He was a mighty king, but he had a kind heart.

"All right then, Lucas," he said, "I suppose you may be friends with Clara. But you're not to make friends with every peasant child in the kingdom of Wrenly."

Prince Lucas ran to his father's arms.

"Thank you, Father," he said. "I promise."

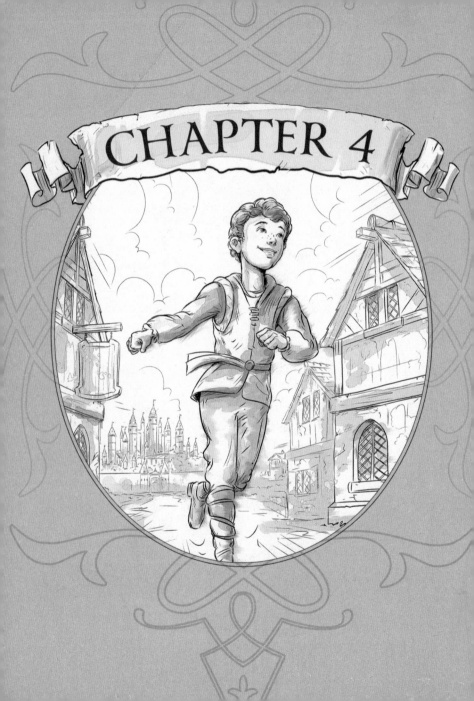

CHAPTER 4

"Hear Ye! Hear Ye!"

Lucas couldn't wait for Clara and her mother to arrive at the palace. So he didn't. He snuck out and raced all the way to the bakery.

Clara always went to the bakery after school. Her father, Owen Gills, worked there.

Lucas peeked down the lane. *The school children are coming!* he thought. He didn't want them to see him, so

he pressed himself against the wall alongside the bakery. Then he listened to what they were saying.

"Why on earth would the prince want to go to school with *us*?" asked a boy named Albin.

"Maybe he's lonely," Clara said. "I

feel sorry for him, cooped up in the castle all day."

The children laughed at Clara.

"How can you feel sorry for the prince?" asked a girl named Martha.

"The prince has everything!" said another girl, named Ashley.

"Not *everything*," said Clara. "He doesn't have a single friend. He's not even allowed to play with me when I visit the palace with my mother."

"Well, I'd trade places with him any day," said Albin. "I'd love to live like a prince."

"I know it sounds like the perfect life," said Clara, "but a palace, fine clothes, and delicious food aren't everything."

Bells jingled as the children stepped into the bakery. Moments later, each child carried a roll of

warm butternut bread to the bench outside. Lucas's mouth watered. How he wished he could join them! As he waited, he heard horses whinny. Then someone began to shout.

"Hear ye! Hear ye!" he cried. "The queen of Wrenly has lost her

prized emerald stone! The king has
offered a grand reward to anyone
who finds it!"

The villagers began to
hurry about to spread
the news.

Oh no! thought
Lucas. *I must get
back to the palace!*

Lucas left his
hiding place and
ran all the way
home, being care-
ful to stay in the
shadows.

CHAPTER 5

A Royal Adventure

Queen Tasha sat at her dressing table, dabbing her eyes with a silk handkerchief. Lucas put his hand on his mother's shoulder. He knew the emerald meant a lot to her. It had belonged to her great-grandmother.

"Don't cry, Mother," he said. "I'm going to find your emerald."

His mother smiled weakly. Then she picked up the gold chain from which her stone no longer dangled.

"It could be anywhere," she said sadly. "I've been all over the king- dom these past two days.

"Where have you traveled to?" Lucas asked.

The queen thought for a moment. "I went to Primlox, Burth, and Hobsgrove," she said.

Lucas sighed.

"You're right. It could be any- where," he said. "But have no fear;

I'm going to find it. I'll need help though."

"What kind of help?" his mother asked.

"Clara's help," said Lucas.

The queen smiled and nodded. "All right," she said. "You have my permission."

"Thank you, Mother," said Lucas. "I *will* find your emerald."

Later that afternoon Clara and her mother arrived at the palace. Lucas grabbed Clara by the hand, and they raced to the royal playroom. Then he told her his idea.

"We'd search for the missing jewel together?" Clara asked.

"Exactly," replied Lucas.

"But will your parents allow it?" asked Clara with a frown.

"They already have after what happened today," said Lucas.

"What do you mean?" Clara asked.

"After I got caught at the school-house, my parents agreed to let us be friends again."

"You mean you didn't get into trouble?" questioned Clara.

"No," said Lucas. "I think they felt sorry for me."

"Why?"

"Because I have no friends," Lucas said.

Clara sat on the swing and looked at Lucas.

"Is it hard being a prince?" asked Clara.

"No, it's D-U-L-L being a prince," said Lucas. "And lonely. I can't even be friends with ordinary children."

"That royally stinks," said Clara.

Lucas laughed. "Well, at least *we* can be friends," he said.

"That's great news," Clara said. "So, when do we start our search?"

"Right now," said Lucas. "And our first adventure will be epic."

"I love epic adventures!" said Clara.

"Then let's make a plan," said Lucas.

Lucas laid out a map of the great kingdom. Then they marked all the places Queen Tasha had been over

the past two days. Clara knew the kingdom of Wrenly well. She had delivered bread to all the lands with her father.

"I'll be your guide," Clara said.

"I can hardly wait," said Lucas.

"How about we meet outside the carriage house after breakfast?"

"There's no school tomorrow so I'll be there," said Clara.

"Can I ask for a small favor?" said Lucas.

"Sure," Clara said.

"Will you bring some butternut bread from the bakery?"

Clara laughed. "Only if you bring me some yummy sausage from the royal pantry," she said.

"Deal," said Lucas.

CHAPTER 6

Rainbow Frost

Wrens, the small brown birds that gave the kingdom its name, twittered in the treetops as Lucas and Clara boarded a royal carriage. They would travel through Flatfrost and over the bridge to the island of Primlox. Lucas stuffed his map of the kingdom in his back pocket—just in case they needed it.

Four magical islands surrounded

Primlox

Hobsgrove

the mainland of Wrenly. Primlox
was ruled by the fairies. Hobsgrove
was known as the island of wizards. The king's dragons roamed
the island of Crestwood, and Burth
belonged to the trolls.

All the islands were protected
by the kingdom of Wrenly, but

Crestwood

Burth

each island was a smaller kingdom
unto itself. King Caleb had to work
very hard to keep the lands united.
Sometimes there was trouble, but for
now all was well.

As the carriage entered Primlox,
Lucas and Clara saw the fairy
queen, Sophie, floating before her

castle. Queen Sophie had shimmering gold wings and a rainbow-jeweled tiara. All the fairies wore clothes made from ferns, feathers, acorns, and flowers. Clara could tell they had used enchanted thread to sew their clothes, because all their outfits sparkled.

Thousands of smooth pebbles formed Queen Sophie's castle. The roof was shingled with shells, and the windows were made of sea glass buffed by the Cobalt Sea. The fairies fluttered toward the carriage.

"Welcome, Prince Lucas," said Queen Sophie.

"Thank you," said Lucas. "This is my friend, Clara. We've come in search of my mother's lost emerald. She said she visited Primlox just yesterday."

"I'm saddened to hear of her loss.

Follow us, and we'll help you retrace her steps."

Lucas and Clara followed the fairies along a path. They crossed over an arched bridge and into the Garden of Strawberries. All the fruit in the kingdom of Wrenly was grown in Primlox. But Primlox was also known for its sweet orange blossom honey.

In the middle of the Garden of Strawberries, Clara saw little round tables carved from tree stumps. Braided twig chairs and red-and-white-dotted stools made of mushrooms surrounded each table.

"Queen Tasha had mint tea and berries in the garden," Queen Sophie said. "She sat over there."

Clara and Lucas began to search for the emerald. They looked around the tables, under the chairs, and throughout the whole garden. But the only thing they found was a ladybug.

"Ladybugs are a sign of good luck,"

said Queen Sophie with a smile.

"We could use a little luck," said Lucas.

"Follow me," said Queen Sophie. "Your mother also strolled through the Maze of Hedges."

"What's the Maze of Hedges?" asked Clara.

"It's a maze formed by many rows of trimmed bushes," Queen Sophie explained.

Lucas and Clara stepped into the maze. They followed a path between the hedges. They couldn't see over the tops of the bushes, but that

didn't matter since they had to keep their eyes on the ground.

They zigzagged through the narrow dirt paths in search of the emerald. Sometimes the path led to a dead end. Then they had to turn around and go another way. Sophie and her ladies-in-waiting

flew overhead to help guide them. They wound their way to a fountain at the center of the maze. There was no sign of the emerald. They searched the other part of the maze until they reached the exit. Still no emerald.

Lucas and Clara sat down on some mushroom stools to rest. Four fairies greeted them with a tray of lemonade. A small, nervous-looking fairy named Rainbow Frost fluttered up to Lucas and Clara.

"I may have a clue to finding the lost emerald," said the fairy in a high-pitched voice.

"What is it?" asked Sophie.

"I saw a lovely green stone in the Citrus Grove yesterday. I was going to pick it up, but my hands were sticky from collecting honey. I washed them in the fountain, but

when I returned, the stone was gone."

"Did my mother visit the grove?" asked Lucas.

"I'm afraid not," said Sophie. "But it's possible that a bird may have mistaken the stone for food and dropped it there."

"Oh no!" cried Clara. "That means another bird could have carried the stone anywhere."

"That's true," Rainbow Frost said. "But I'm not sure that's what happened."

"Why not?" asked Lucas.

"Because I saw a big troll in the citrus grove," Rainbow Frost said.

69

"And everyone knows trolls cannot resist treasure."

"Do you know his name?" Clara asked.

"His name is Hambone," the fairy said.

"We must leave for Burth at once!" declared Lucas.

"Let's go!" Clara said.

Queen Sophie loaned Lucas and Clara a boat to sail to Burth quickly. She also gave them a bundle of treats, which Clara tucked into her satchel. Lucas and Clara thanked the fairies and waved good-bye.

CHAPTER 7

Hambone

Nobody greeted Lucas and Clara on the island of Burth. The trolls were neither friendly nor outgoing. They worked hard and grew vegetables for the entire kingdom. The kids walked to the stables in the village. Lucas tapped a sleeping troll on the shoulder.

The troll snorted and rubbed his eyes. "What do you want?" he grumbled, with one eye closed.

"We'd like to hire a horse," said Lucas.

"What for?" asked the troll.

"To visit a troll called Hambone," said Lucas. "Do you know where he lives?"

"Pay up," said the troll.

Lucas dropped a coin in the troll's grubby hand.

The troll smiled and bit the coin. "He lives on Old Tinder Road. His door is marked by the sign of a crescent moon," said the troll. "And don't tell him I sent you."

So Lucas and Clara mounted the horse and galloped along the rugged valley floor. Steep, craggy mountains towered over the island of Burth. The air smelled of garlic. They passed fields of corn, rows of turnips, and gardens of parsley. Soon the road began to go up. It twisted

around and around a mountain-side. Lucas and Clara passed cave dwellings all along the way.

"Whoa, back!" Clara cried as she jerked the reins. "We just passed a crescent moon!"

They tied the horse to a hitching post and knocked on the cave door

marked with the crescent moon. A potbellied troll with green eyes and wild gray hair answered the door. He looked Lucas and Clara up and down.

"We came for Queen Tasha's lost emerald," said Lucas. "Do you have it?"

The troll recognized the boy as the prince. He knew better than to play games with the son of the king.

"I found it in the Citrus Grove when I was gathering oranges," said Hambone.

Big grins spread across Lucas's and Clara's faces.

"But I no longer have it," he said gruffly. "I traded it for some hair-smoothing potion."

Lucas's smile disappeared. "So who has it now?"

"A wizard," said Hambone.

"Which one?" Lucas demanded.

"A wizard named Olaf," said the troll. "Now be off!"

And he shut the door with a thump.

"Looks like this adventure is far from over!" cried Lucas. "To Hobsgrove!"

Lucas and Clara raced back to the dock, boarded their ship, and sailed to Hobsgrove, the island of wizards.

CHAPTER 8

Olaf

The ship sailed past the island of Crestwood. Dragons played on the hillsides and soared overhead. Some snoozed in caves and some under the trees of the Great Pine Forest. A volcano puffed steam from the center of the island.

Soon the ship docked at Hobsgrove. A thick cloud of fog hung over the island. Even when

it was sunny everywhere else, Hobsgrove was always gray.

Ivy creeped up the dark walls and spires of the castle, where André and Grom, the two brothers who ruled Hobsgrove, lived. André was known to be very kind and friendly, but

Grom was not. He liked to keep to himself and spent most of his time in the dreary castle basement, mixing potions.

Many of the wizards on the island of Hobsgrove worked by the hearths of their thatched-roof homes. Their cauldrons bubbled with magical

healing potions made for the kingdom of Wrenly.

A young wizard brought Lucas

and Clara to Olaf's dark, smoky house. Olaf stood over his cauldron as it foamed and frothed. Lucas asked the black-bearded wizard if he had the missing emerald. The wizard shook his head glumly.

"No," he said. "That dreadful witch from Bogburp cursed me with clumsiness years ago."

"What does that have to do with the missing emerald?" asked Clara.

The wizard looked at them with sad brown eyes.

"The emerald fell from my hand after I returned home from Burth. It tumbled over Hob's Cliff and into the sea."

"Oh no!" Lucas cried. "That emerald belonged to my mother, Queen Tasha."

"That's most unfortunate," said the wizard. "Do tell her I'm sorry."

Lucas kicked a stone on the path as he and Clara headed back to the dock. "What are we going to do *now?*" he asked. "Go diving for it?"

"I have a better idea," said Clara. "Let's go to Mermaid's Cove."

"What for?"

"So we can leave a message in the sand for the mermaids," replied Clara.

"And how is *that* going to help?"

"Maybe the mermaids can find the emerald," she explained. "They always find the most beautiful shells and leave them on the beach for me."

"And how do you know it's the mermaids and not the tides?" Lucas asked.

"Because the shells are polished and perfect. None of them have been broken by the rocks and waves."

Lucas sighed and looked toward the mainland.

"It's worth a try," said Clara.

"I suppose," Lucas said.

So they boarded their ship and headed for Mermaid's Cove.

91

CHAPTER 9

Mermaid Magic

At Mermaid's Cove, the pink coral sand sparkled in the afternoon sun. Lucas and Clara kicked off their shoes and walked along the beach, looking for the perfect spot.

"Here's a good place," said Clara as she got down on her knees.

Lucas looked on as Clara wrote a message in the sand with a thin stick.

Dear mermaids,

Queen Tasha's emerald is lost in the sea off Hob's Cliff. Can you help us find it? Thank you for all the beautiful shells.

Love,

Your friend Clara

Lucas laughed. "You're crazy," he said.

Clara laughed. "I'm also hungry. Let's have our picnic."

Clara unwrapped the treats that the fairies had given them. Then she and Lucas sat by the far end of the cove. They talked and laughed and nibbled on bread, cheese, and grapes.

Lucas smiled at Clara. "I may

not have found my mother's emerald," he said, "but I have found one thing."

"What?" asked Clara.

"A real friend," Lucas said.

"Me too," said Clara. "I'm glad we can spend time together."

Lucas nodded. "We'd better get going. The sun's starting to set."

Lucas and Clara dipped their toes in the water as they walked down the beach.

"Look at your message," said Lucas. "It's already been washed away by the tide."

"Shall I write it again?" asked Clara.

"No, let's just head home," Lucas said. "We can come back tomorrow."

They sat on a rock to put on their shoes, but some shells caught Clara's attention. "Wow, these are beautiful," she said.

Lucas looked at a cluster of shells,

perfectly displayed on the sand.

"Were the shells here when we arrived?" he asked.

"No," said Clara. Her eyes grew wide. "The mermaids!"

"Mermaids again?" asked Lucas.

"I'm serious!" said Clara as she gently placed a shell in her satchel.

Clara loved to collect seashells.

"But we've been on the beach the whole time," said Lucas. "And we didn't see a single mermaid."

"Well," said Clara, "mermaids are very sly."

She picked up a half-open scallop shell and peeked inside.

"They're so sly that I've never ever seen one," said Lucas.

Clara handed the shell to Lucas.

"It's pretty," he said.

"Open it," said Clara.

Lucas opened the shell. He expected to see a clump of sand. But he saw something else.

"My mother's emerald!" he cried. "How could it be?"

"Mermaids," said Clara.

Lucas gazed out to sea. Then he looked at the emerald.

He couldn't believe it.

"Okay!" he shouted to the sea. "I believe!"

Lucas ran back to the shore and stooped to write in the sand.

Dear mermaids,

Thank you for finding my mother's emerald. Clara and I hope to meet you someday.

Your friends,

Prince Lucas and Clara Gills

Lucas put the emerald in his pocket. Clara placed the empty scallop shell in her satchel.

"For my collection," she said with a smile.

"I never would've found this without you," he said.

"What are friends for?" Clara asked.

Lucas smiled. "Race you to the palace!"

Then they quickly put on their shoes, and ran off.

CHAPTER 10

Scallop

Lucas and Clara burst into the palace's great hall. King Caleb and Queen Tasha looked up from their chess game.

"What's all the fuss?" asked the startled king.

Lucas reached into his pocket and wrapped his fingers around the emerald.

"We have a very special present

for Mother," he said excitedly.

Lucas pulled his fist out of his pocket. Then he opened his hand to reveal the emerald.

Queen Tasha put her hand to her heart.

"Oh, you precious, brave, wonderful boy!" she exclaimed.

"It wasn't me, Mother," said Lucas. "Clara found it."

"We *both* did," Clara said.

"It was a real royal goose chase," Lucas added. "But Clara was the one who actually found it. She's very clever, Mother."

"Thank you, Clara," said the queen.

Clara curtsied.

King Caleb was very grateful. "You shall receive a handsome reward," he said. "Follow me."

Lucas, Clara, and Queen Tasha followed King Caleb through a heavy oak door and down a spiral stone staircase. They walked all the way to the royal stables. The king stopped in front of a stall. A beautiful brown horse with a black mane, black tail, white socks, and black hooves whinnied at them.

"Clara, this is your reward," said the king.

Clara gasped.

"You may ride her whenever you visit the palace."

"She's beautiful!" cried Clara as she pet the horse's mane. "Thank you, King Caleb."

"What would you like to call her?" asked the king.

Clara looked into the horse's eyes.

"I'd like to call her Scallop," she said. "Because we found the emerald in a scallop shell."

"A very good choice," said the king. Then he put his arms around Lucas and Clara. "I owe you two an apology. I'm sorry I didn't let you play together before."

"That's okay," Clara said.

"We know it's hard being a king," Lucas added.

The king and queen laughed. Then they went back to the palace.

Clara linked her arm with Lucas's. "Hey, friend—will you go riding with me?"

Lucas smiled. "I sure will."

Hear ye! Hear ye!
Presenting the next book from
The Kingdom of Wrenly!
Here's a sneak peek!

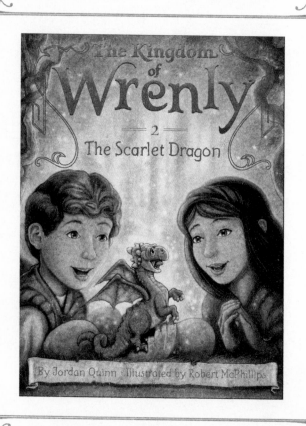

Lucas spotted Clara outside a stall. He watched her gently brush her horse, Scallop. The horse had been a reward from King Caleb for finding Queen Tasha's lost emerald.

"Clara!" called Lucas. "You'll never guess what!"

Clara's green eyes lit up when she saw her friend. "What?" she asked.

"André and Grom found a red dragon's egg on Crestwood!" said Lucas.

"A red dragon's egg!" exclaimed Clara. "Do you know what that means?"

Excerpt from *The Scarlet Dragon*

"It means there's a scarlet dragon inside!"

"Exactly," said Clara. Then her face became serious. "And you know what they say about red dragons."

"Sure," answered Lucas. "The legends say they're the most magnificent dragons in all the world!"

"And the most feared," Clara added.

"Not to worry," Lucas said. "It's all in the training."

Clara rolled her eyes and sighed. "Lucas, have you ever trained a fire-breathing dragon?" she asked.

Excerpt from *The Scarlet Dragon*

"Actually, I've never even trained a dog," Lucas said. "But the knights and wizards know all about dragon training."

"I suppose," said Clara. "But there's never been a fire-breathing dragon in the kingdom before. What if it sets Wrenly on fire?"

"Then we'll put the fire out," said Lucas. "Trust me. A red dragon is going to be amazing."

Excerpt from *The Scarlet Dragon*

Look for these other Little Simon chapter books!

   HEiDi HECKELBECK

the CRiTTER club

GREETINGS FROM SOMEWHERE